*For all the children who can't
hug the ones they love.*

P.D. and E.M.

Eoin McLaughlin 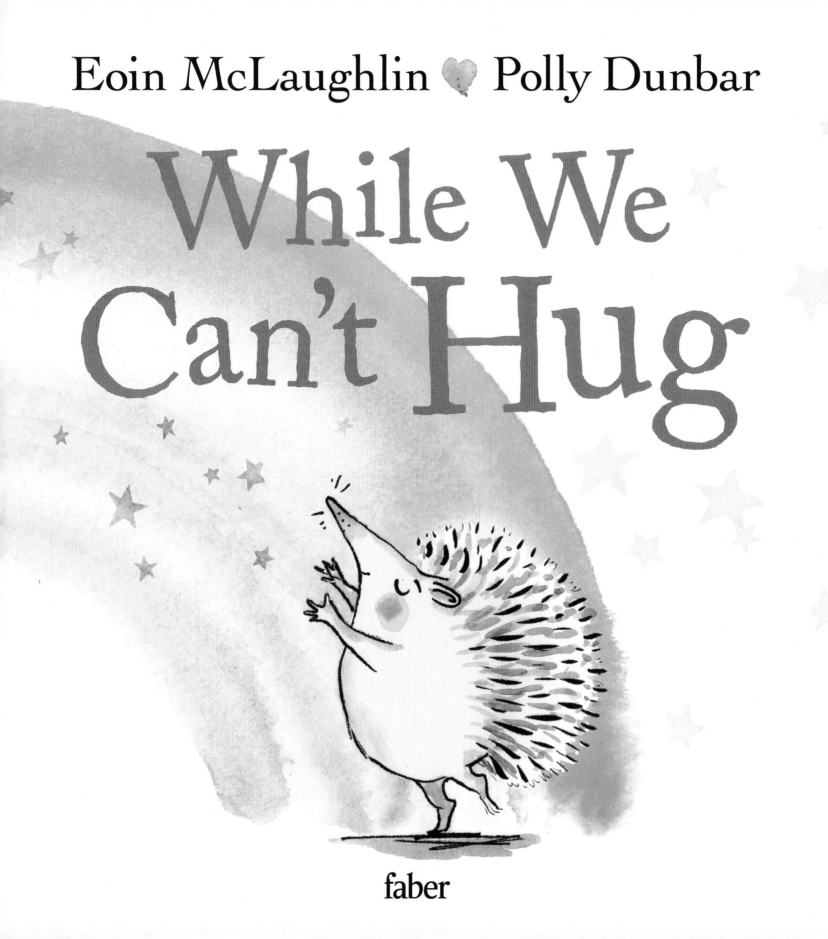 Polly Dunbar

While We Can't Hug

faber

Hedgehog and Tortoise were the best of friends.
They wanted to give each other a great, big hug.

But they weren't allowed to touch.

"Don't worry," said Owl.
"There are lots of ways
to show someone you
love them."

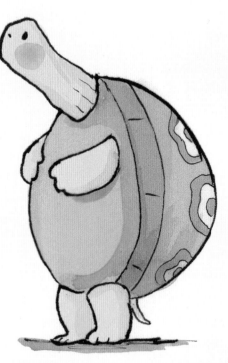

Hedgehog tried a wave.

That made Tortoise smile.

Tortoise made a funny face.
That made Hedgehog laugh.

Hedgehog wrote a letter.

And Tortoise wrote one back.

And when Tortoise did a little dance,
Hedgehog joined in, too.

Hedgehog blew a kiss

across the gap

between

them.

Tortoise saw it, and caught it, and kept it.

And sent three back again.

Tortoise sang a song.
Hedgehog played along.

Then they both painted pictures,

so that everyone would know they
were friends . . .

. . . through rain . . .

. . . and shine.

They could not touch.

They could not hug.

But they both knew

that they were loved.

Faber has published children's books since 1929.
T. S. Eliot's *Old Possum's Book of Practical Cats*
and Ted Hughes' *The Iron Man* were amongst
the first. Our catalogue at the time said that
'it is by reading such books that children learn
the difference between the shoddy and the
genuine'. We still believe in the power of reading
to transform children's lives. All our books are
chosen with the express intention of growing
a love of reading, a thirst for knowledge and
to cultivate empathy. We pride ourselves on
responsible editing. Last but not least, we believe
in kind and inclusive books in which all children
feel represented and important.

First published in the UK in 2020
First published in the US in 2020
by Faber and Faber Limited
Bloomsbury House, 74–77 Great Russell Street, London WC1B 3DA
Text © Eoin McLaughlin, 2020 Illustrations © Polly Dunbar, 2020
Designed by Faber and Faber
HB ISBN 978–0–571–36558–6
PB ISBN 978–0–571–36560–9
Printed in the UK
10 9 8 7 6 5 4 3
The moral rights of Eoin McLaughlin and Polly Dunbar have been asserted.
A CIP record for this book is available from the British Library.